THE LEGENDS OF KING ARTHUR

MERLIN, MAGIC AND DRAGONS

CB007131

Dados Internacionais de Catalogação na Publicação (CIP) de acordo com ISBD

M469s   Mayhew, Tracey
        The sword in the stone / adaptado por Tracey Mayhew. – Jandira : W. Books, 2025.
        96 p. ; 12,8cm x 19,8cm. – (The legends of king Arthur)

        ISBN: 978-65-5294-164-0

        1. Literatura infantojuvenil. 2. Literatura Infantil. 3. Clássicos. 4. Literatura inglesa. 5. Lendas. 6. Folclore. 7. Mágica. 8. Cultura Popular. I. Título. II. Série.

2025-619   CDD 028.5
                                                CDU 82-93

Elaborado por Vagner Rodolfo da Silva - CRB-8/9410
Índice para catálogo sistemático:
1. Literatura infantojuvenil 028.5
2. Literatura infantojuvenil 82-93

The Legends of King Arthur: Merlin, Magic, and Dragons
Text © Sweet Cherry Publishing Limited, 2020
Inside illustrations © Sweet Cherry Publishing Limited, 2020
Cover illustrations © Sweet Cherry Publishing Limited, 2020

Text by Tracey Mayhew
Illustrations by Mike Phillips

© 2025 edition:
Ciranda Cultural Editora e Distribuidora Ltda.

1st edition in 2025
www.cirandacultural.com.br

THE LEGENDS OF KING ARTHUR

THE SWORD IN THE STONE

Retold by
Tracey Mayhew

Illustrated by
Mike Phillips

W. Books

Chapter One

Arthur was exhausted. He had spent the day following his brother around town as they sold the grain and eggs their father had given them that morning.

As usual, Kay had taken the opportunity to visit every blacksmith along the way, admiring all the new weapons and armour.

Arthur wasn't interested in swords or bows, but he enjoyed Kay's excitement as the older boy tested the weight and balance of each. Arthur could almost see Kay's mind working as he imagined himself wearing this or that shining helmet, wielding one gleaming blade or another.

'One day, Arthur,' Kay swore, as he put back a spear even taller than he was. 'One day I'll be a Knight of the Realm. I'll serve the king. I'll fight for Britain!'

As they walked home, Kay lopped the heads off of weeds growing along their path with a stick. It cut more cleanly than the battered sword that hung at his side did. That one had previously belonged to their father.

'When we have a king again,' Kay continued, 'he'll need loyal knights to help him defeat the brigands–' *swish* '–and warlords–' *chop* '–who terrorise the land. Together we'll bring peace!'

Arthur didn't like to remind Kay that Britain had been without a king for so many years now, it was doubtful that they would ever have another. As for peace, it was a thing that didn't even exist in their father's stories.

Arthur and Kay's childhood had been spent listening to Sir Ector's tales of King Uther Pendragon. He told them how brave and strong he had been as a ruler. Yet King Uther's reign had hardly been what Arthur would call peaceful, and it had ended without an heir to inherit his throne. Arthur doubted anyone would be brave enough, or stupid enough, to rule now.

Whilst its own people fought each other over a crown, foreign invaders had begun to advance with their sights set on Britain herself.

'I promise you, brother,' Kay repeated. '*One day.*'

Arthur rolled his eyes. 'I know, I know: one day you'll be sitting beside the king himself.' Kay cuffed him

gently, but it still sent Arthur reeling into the tall grass. His brother would make a fearsome knight.

'And you?' Kay laughed, pulling Arthur back onto the path. 'What will you be doing? A noble knight needs a loyal squire, you know.'

Arthur shook his head. Whether he believed it would happen or not, Kay was born to be a knight. He had all the right qualities: he was brave and strong and true. Arthur was …

'A farmer,' he declared. 'Whilst you are sitting beside the king, I will be growing crops and tending animals. *Not* wondering if I will survive the day.'

Kay grinned. 'Father will be pleased to hear that. At least one of his sons will carry on his good name.' He glanced at Arthur. 'You're not cut out for battle anyway.'

Arthur ignored the sting. He knew his brother was right, but it didn't make the words hurt any less. He and Kay couldn't have been more different. Kay was bigger and more muscular.

He enjoyed learning to fight and to find the weakness in a suit of armour. Arthur was skinny, and took no pleasure in either. But despite their differences, and Kay's constant teasing, Arthur knew that they would always be there for each other, no matter what.

As they rounded the final bend before their family farm, they stopped. Up ahead, an old man holding a wooden staff stood by a rickety cart. His horse nervously pawed at the ground, whilst three men raided the goods he carried.

Instantly, Kay's hand flew to the sword at his side, but Arthur grabbed his arm before he could pull the

weapon free. Kay glared. 'What are you doing?' he demanded angrily, trying to shake himself free.

Arthur only tightened his grip. 'Stopping you before you do something stupid!'

Finally, pulling himself free, Kay moved away from Arthur, sword sliding from scabbard. 'What would you rather we do, Arthur? Hide whilst they steal from an old man?'

Guilt flooded Arthur: how could he even think about running away when a poor old man was being robbed right in front of them? Swallowing hard instead, Arthur looked to Kay. 'What should we do?' he whispered urgently.

Thankfully the robbers were far too preoccupied with the old man to notice two boys on the road ahead. 'First of all, you need a weapon.' Kay handed his sword to Arthur before pulling a dagger free from his belt.

Looking down at the nicked blade in his hand and then back to Kay, Arthur said, 'But … this is yours. Father gave it to you.'

'Just follow me and remember what Father and I have taught you.'

Arthur nodded, but his mind had gone blank. What had they taught him? Kay grinned. 'And, if all else fails, just keep swinging until you hit something. Just make sure you don't hit *me*.'

With that, Kay raced towards the cart, his dagger held high, screaming a war cry that could strike fear into the heart of even the bravest knight.

Surprised, the men – boys, it turned out – stopped looting. They turned to see Kay charging towards them. Leaping from the cart, the smaller two disappeared into the trees, whilst the biggest jumped down and drew a sword.

Arthur's blood ran cold as he watched his brother closing in with

only a dagger. Without thinking, Arthur raised Kay's sword and charged, echoing his cry. There was fear in the boy's eyes, but it was quickly replaced with determination. He faced his attacker, blade now raised to meet Kay's.

It was too late. Arthur would never make it in time …

Suddenly, moving faster than Arthur would have thought possible, the old

man stepped forwards. Reaching out,
he tripped the boy with his staff. The
boy fell face first in the dirt, rolled,
and came up spluttering, desperately
clawing at the ground for his blade. Kay
was already kicking it out of his reach.

'Think it's brave to pick on an old man, do you?' he demanded, as Arthur skidded to a stop beside him.

'I-I'm sorry!' the boy cried, his eyes wide. 'I was just–'

Kay turned away, fixing his attention on the old man, who was now leaning on the cart. 'Are you well, sir?'

The old man nodded. 'Thanks to you two brave souls,' he wheezed, glancing between them.

Arthur blushed, embarrassed by his share in the praise. He had done nothing to deserve it.

Kay looked back down at the boy on the ground. 'Get out of here,' he spat, nudging him with his foot. Nodding, the boy scrambled to his feet, eager to put as much distance between himself and Kay as possible.

'He forgot his sword,' Arthur pointed out.

Kay's eyes lit up. 'My sword now,' he announced, retrieving the weapon from the ground and gazing at it lovingly. At the same time, Arthur bent down and fetched the old man's fallen staff.

'Here you are,' he offered.

The man took it. 'Thank you, dear boy.'

'I'm Arthur, and this is my brother, Kay.'

'I am Emrys,' the old man replied, drawing his threadbare cloak around him as he circled his cart.

'You shouldn't travel alone, Emrys,' Arthur said, realising that the old man intended to continue his journey. 'It's not safe.'

Emrys's eyes twinkled. 'Then I shall hope to meet other brave souls, like yourselves, to help me.'

Arthur frowned. He couldn't let the old man go when he had just been attacked. 'Our farm is only a little way from here. You could spend the night with us and rest before continuing on your way tomorrow.'

'Arthur,' Kay warned quietly, 'we barely have enough food to feed *ourselves*.'

'Our father won't mind,' Arthur insisted, ignoring him. He gestured to the old man's horse. 'It looks like your mare could do with a rest.'

Emrys sighed. 'I'm sure she could ...' He patted the animal and smiled suddenly at Arthur. 'As could I!'

You do your father proud by taking pity on an old man. And don't worry about the food,' he added to Kay. 'I have food that I would gladly share with you and your family.'

'Then it's decided,' Arthur declared. 'You're coming home with us.'

The man's smile widened. 'Lead the way!'

Chapter Two

'A *tournament*?' Kay repeated, still awestruck by the idea.

Emrys smiled, sipping wine from his cup. 'The largest tournament you could imagine.'

Kay shook his head in wonder – he could imagine a very large tournament indeed!

'And in two days' time,' Emrys continued, 'men and boys from around the country will be competing to win it.'

'What happens if they do?' Arthur asked around a hunk of cheese.

Emrys had provided them with a small feast!

'Then they win the crown, too,' Emrys announced.

Arthur swallowed his mouthful. 'What about the sword in the stone?'

'What about it?' Ector asked quietly. He had been quiet since their return, his own wine still untouched.

'I thought only the one who freed the sword could be king?'

'It's been years since Uther died,' Ector reminded him. 'Many have tried to free the sword since then. None have succeeded. It is time to try another way.'

'It's true,' Emrys agreed, speaking carefully. 'So far no one has proved worthy to pull the sword from the stone.'

Kay stood abruptly, almost upsetting the table along with his chair.

'Kay!' Ector cried, reaching out to stop his cup from spilling.

'I'm sorry, Father,' Kay gasped, but he did not sit back down. He stared at Emrys. 'So whoever wins the tournament will be king?' he demanded. '*King of Britain*?'

Emrys nodded. 'Indeed.'

Kay spun excitedly towards Ector. 'Father! You know what this means, don't you? It means we have to go to–' He glanced at Emrys uncertainly.

'Londinium,' Emrys supplied with a smile.

'We *have* to go to Londinium!' Kay cried.

Ector raised an eyebrow. 'And who will look after the farm whilst we are gone?'

'It doesn't matter! Father, this is my chance! *I* could be the one to win the tournament – or if not I can serve the man who does!'

Ector shook his head. 'I'm sorry, Kay, but–'

'This is not a chance that should be passed up,' Emrys interrupted.

'Please, Father,' Kay begged.

'King or knight,' Ector murmured, his eyes darting between Kay and Arthur, 'it would be a dangerous life.'

'But a worthy one,' Kay argued.

Emrys smiled at Kay. 'As you have shown yourself to be a worthy young man.'

Ector sighed. 'You won't give up until I say yes, will you?' The words seemed meant for Kay, but Ector's eyes had once again shifted to Emrys. After a moment, he sighed heavily.

'Very well. We leave for Londinium in the morning.'

Kay punched the air in victory. 'Thank you, Father!' he cried. 'I will go and pack. I'll be ready at first light!'

And with that, he was gone.

Emrys cleared his throat in the quiet that followed. 'And you, Arthur? Have you any interest in entering the tournament?'

Arthur nearly choked on his drink, glad that Kay wasn't there to laugh at the suggestion. '*Me*?' he spluttered.

'You've never dreamt of being a knight like your brother? A king, even?'

Arthur shook his head vigorously. 'Never.'

'Why is that? I saw your bravery on the road. You are just as worthy as he is.'

'I wasn't brave! I was terrified. I couldn't lead anyone.'

'No man ever really knows what he can do, until he does it,' Emrys pointed out.

'Enough!' Ector cried suddenly, startling them. 'You cannot force him to do something he doesn't want to!'

Emrys leant forwards in his chair, equally fierce now. 'And you cannot deny him a chance to fulfil his destiny.'

Arthur laughed to break the sudden tension. What were they even arguing about?

'My *destiny* is to stay here, at the farm,' he announced firmly. 'After Kay has beaten or *talked* his opponents into submission at the tournament, that is.'

No one else laughed at the joke, and Arthur found himself eager to leave. 'I should go and pack for the journey, too,' he excused himself. 'Goodnight.'

Both men's eyes seemed to follow Arthur as he left the room. Remembering how Ector's face had paled when he'd seen their guest, Arthur couldn't help feeling like there was something important he was missing. But what?

Chapter Three

Arthur had just loaded his bag onto his father's cart in the morning when Kay arrived, dropping his own at Arthur's feet. Arthur looked down at it before looking questioningly at Kay.

'Well, if you're going to be my squire …' Kay began.

Arthur frowned. 'Who said I was?'

Kay grinned, throwing an arm around Arthur's shoulders. 'Arthur, I cannot arrive in Londinium without a squire. Who would take me seriously?'

'But why does it have to be me?'

'Because you're my little brother and you want me to win.' Arthur sighed, shaking his head as he bent to pick up the bag. 'Oh, and you're in charge of my sword, too,' Kay added, slipping the scabbard from his belt and handing it to Arthur.

'See that you keep it well-oiled and sharp,' he instructed before mounting his horse. He had insisted on arriving on horseback rather than sharing the cart. The animal pranced with his excitement. 'And don't lose it!' he called back with a laugh.

Arthur bit his tongue, fighting the urge to remind Kay that he didn't know how to look after a sword.

Ector climbed onto the cart. 'Right, then. Unless you two have forgotten anything ...'

Arthur looked around for Emrys and saw his cart pulling out ahead of them.

Ector snapped the reins and their horse began to follow slowly, then gradually to pick up speed. Looking back, Arthur felt a stirring of excitement. The farmhouse grew smaller and smaller in the distance. The furthest he had ever been from home had been the nearest town. Londinium would be a whole new adventure.

'Arthur!' Kay hissed. 'Are you asleep?'

'Yes,' Arthur mumbled. As if the constant jolting of the cart would let him sleep! Boring though the journey was. Similar – and numerous! – though the fields and trees along the way had been. And despite Kay droning on and on about what would happen when he drew the sword from the stone–

Arthur yawned hugely.

'Arthur!'

'What?' He looked around. 'Where are we?' The light was fading and it was colder now. The landscape finally looked different; shadowed and gloomy.

Arthur shivered and reached for his cloak.

Kay shook his head, pulling his own furs around his shoulders. 'I don't know. When we stop, I'll teach you how to use a whetstone. I can't have my squire looking like he doesn't know what he's doing, can I?'

It wasn't long before their father found a place to sleep for the night. Arthur and Emrys set up camp, whilst Ector and Kay used the last of the light to hunt their supper. Kay had talked so loudly as they headed off that it would be a miracle if they caught anything.

'Your brother seems very sure of himself,' Emrys observed, as they sat beside the fire they had built.

'He is,' Arthur chuckled affectionately. 'He'll make a great leader.'

'But not you?'

Arthur shook his head. 'I'm not like Kay.'

'In what way?'

'In every way! Kay's strong. He always knows what to do, even if it doesn't always turn out well. He's easily the best fighter in the village. I can barely even hold a sword!'

Emrys studied him for a long moment, the firelight playing across his face. 'You know, there are many

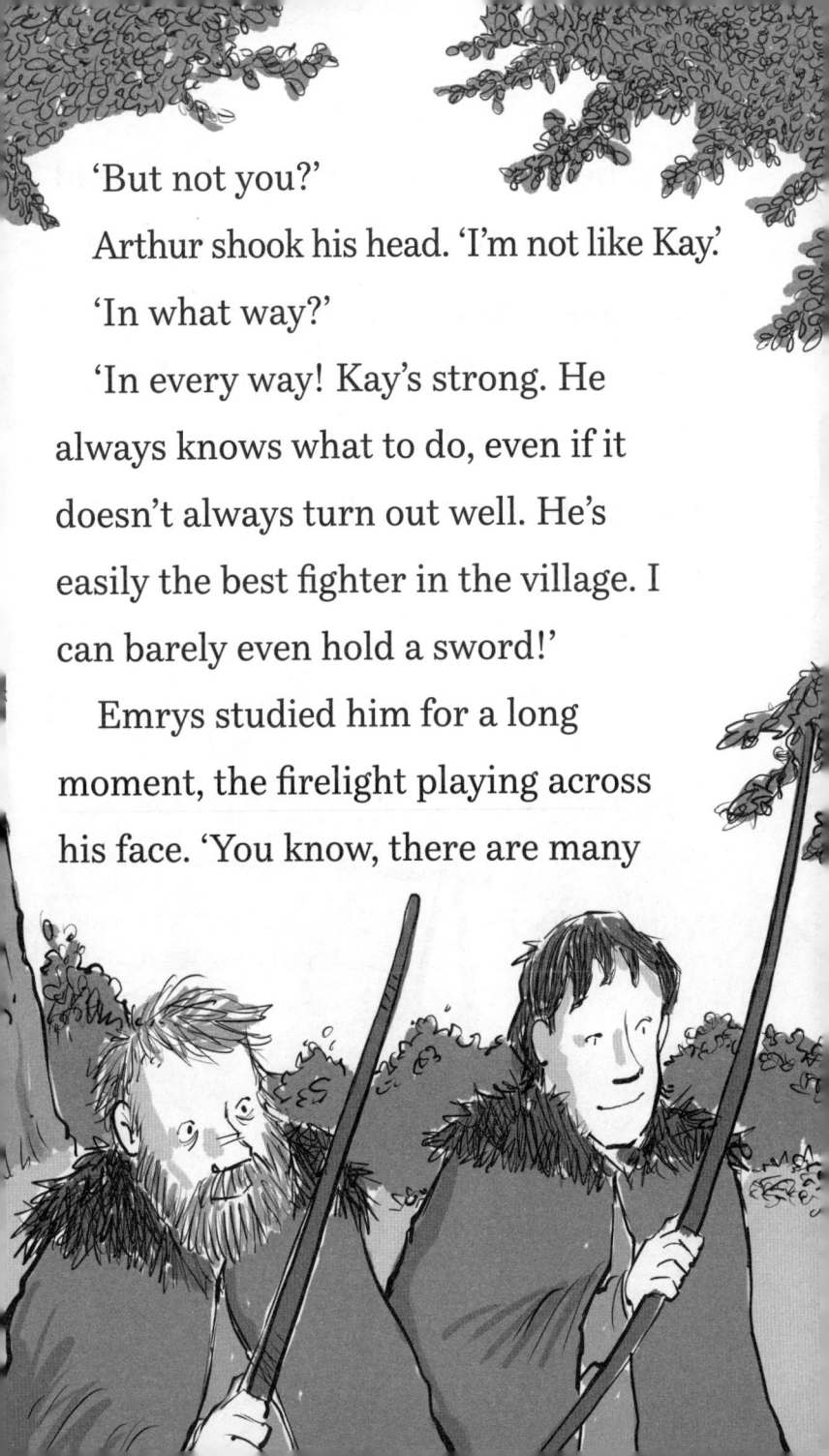

qualities that make men worthy to lead others. Just because you cannot use a sword does not make you weak. There are many qualities *you* possess, Arthur, that Kay does not. You are humble and honest. Brave, too, when you need to be.' He smiled as he continued, 'And

it is wise to remember that, whilst you can *learn* to fight, not everyone possesses the other qualities.'

Arthur blushed and was relieved when Kay and Ector appeared from the trees carrying two hares, their bows slung over their shoulders.

'Supper!' Kay declared triumphantly, as he dropped his hare onto a rock near the fire. 'I caught the bigger one,' he boasted. 'It tried to get away but I was too quick for it!'

At these words, Emrys caught Arthur's eye. *See*? his look seemed to say. It left Arthur feeling uneasy.

Later that night, Arthur awoke to the sound
of hushed voices coming from the other
side of the campfire. Kay was asleep on his
left, snoring softly under his blanket.

It was his father's voice that Arthur
could hear. It sounded angry.

'I've already told you; he's too young
for any of this,' Ector was saying.

'Need I remind you, Ector,' Emrys replied, surprising Arthur with his familiar tone, 'that this is his destiny. He was born to lead.'

There was a moment's silence before Ector spoke again. 'I don't like it. Any of it.'

'You don't have to like it. You just have to accept it.'

Movement appeared in Arthur's line of sight as Ector marched across the camp to his bedroll. He closed his eyes quickly, heart pounding. That night, he lay awake for hours, replaying their conversation, until sleep finally claimed him.

Chapter Four

There was a strange atmosphere in camp the following morning. Ector and Emrys barely looked at each other, let alone spoke, whilst Kay was lost in his own thoughts. Today they would arrive in Londinium, and Arthur knew that Kay was growing nervous. Despite all his boasting, he had never had to compete with anyone for anything before.

As they continued their journey, Arthur tried his best to keep Kay distracted, but it soon became clear that he was not interested in talking – even about himself.

By silent agreement, the group did not stop to eat or rest, but rode onwards. When they reached Londinium, Arthur was both relieved and amazed. It was so busy! After a quiet life in the country, he could not believe all the sights, sounds and smells. Merchants called out, selling

their wares. Small children ran about, their laughter shrill to Arthur's ears.

Cooking fires had been set up between tents raised for the tournament. Many of them bore the coat of arms of their inhabitants. Scarred warriors prowled the streets, weapons strapped to their hips and backs, their eyes watchful.

Seeing them, Arthur couldn't help wondering if Kay would be competing against such men tomorrow.

Eventually their path widened into a clearing even more busy than the market and camps behind. Until the way ahead was blocked entirely by a large crowd, talking excitedly and straining their necks.

'There it is!' Kay cried, standing in his stirrups and pointing over their heads.

Arthur stood on the hay bail in the back of the cart and shaded his eyes. He gasped.

The sword was half swallowed by rock, but the blade glinted in the sun, casting shards of light across the creeping moss and lichen. It looked like it had been there forever.

Arthur had never seen anything so beautiful.

'Father, stop!' Kay cried, pulling his horse in beside the cart. By the time Ector had brought them to a standstill, Kay had dismounted, thrown the reins at Arthur, and disappeared into the crowd.

When the horses were tethered, Arthur, Ector and Emrys found Kay standing at the front of the vast crowd, at the base of the enormous rock, gazing up, up, up in wonder.

'Isn't it beautiful?' he breathed.

Emrys looked at Arthur, who could only nod in agreement.

The simple pommel and cross guard shone brightly, calling out to every man and boy in the crowd, offering them a future equally golden. Even Arthur, with no love of swords in general, felt drawn to this one in particular. He understood the people in the crowd who goaded each other on to try drawing it for themselves, until, despite the tournament, an unruly queue had formed. As Arthur watched, a mountain of a man climbed onto the rock, but after straining and pulling until his muscles bulged, the sword did not budge.

'You feel it, don't you?' Emrys murmured, still watching Arthur closely. 'It's calling to you.'

Arthur frowned and shook his head. 'I don't know what you mean.' Turning his back on the old man and the sword, he walked over to his brother, whose voice had risen above the murmur of the crowd.

'That sword is mine!' Kay declared.

Another boy, wearing a leather breastplate, laughed harshly. 'If you think *you* stand a chance, farm boy, then think again,' he sneered.

'What's that supposed to mean?' Kay shot back, rounding on his opponent.

'It means I'll beat you in the tournament tomorrow and come back here to claim the sword.' The boy pointed with as much confidence as Kay.

'Why don't you try claiming it now?'

'Why don't you?'

A voice came from the crowd. 'Why don't *both* of you?'

Both boys realised then that they had an audience, and not a friendly one. Many there had tried and failed to free the sword already, and it was clear to Arthur that neither his brother nor

his new "friend" wanted to risk failing in front of them.

'After the tournament,' they agreed, gruffly.

Many members of the crowd laughed.

'When *I* have been proved worthy,' Kay muttered as he stalked off in his own direction, Arthur scrambling to keep up.

'Are you aware that you just vowed to win the tournament and pull the sword from the stone,' he gasped, 'in front of *everyone*?'

'Yes.'

'And you aren't afraid you're wrong?'

'No.'

Kay stopped so suddenly that Arthur slammed into his back. 'I have faith in my abilities, brother. I know I am a good fighter, and I know I am worthy to claim that sword as my own.' He grinned. 'I just have to prove it.'

Despite feeling Kay's share of fear on top of his own, Arthur had to smile too. Emrys was right: Kay certainly wasn't humble.

Chapter Five

The following morning was cloudy and grey. It had rained for most of the night, leaving everything damp and soggy.

Arthur crawled out of their tent, shivering in the early morning light,

and breathed in the sharp, acrid smoke from the fires. Most people were already awake, including Ector and Kay who were sitting quietly by the fire.

Ector was staring into the flames, prodding the embers with a thick branch. He looked tired, as if he hadn't slept. Arthur could see the worry on his face. He understood it perfectly: neither of them wanted to see Kay hurt in the tournament.

Kay looked no better. He was frowning, his face pale and tense. His breakfast sat untouched beside him on the ground.

As Arthur approached, Ector looked up and forced a smile. 'Good morning, son,' he murmured.

'Morning, Father.' Arthur glanced at Kay. 'How are you feeling?'

Kay didn't meet his eyes as he replied, 'I'm ready for whatever comes my way.'

Ector reached out, placing a hand on Kay's shoulder. 'You will be victorious,' he declared. 'And tonight, we will celebrate.'

Kay nodded and replied more confidently. 'Yes, Father. We will.'

Movement caught Arthur's eye and he turned to find Emrys walking towards them, weaving his way through the campfires, scarcely leaning on his staff.

He smiled as he drew close. 'The crowds are gathering. We should leave now.'

Kay stood abruptly. 'Then what are we waiting for?'

'That shield's seen better days, farm boy!'

Kay glared as they passed the boy he had argued with the previous day. 'I'll make him sorry he ever laughed at me!' he growled so that only Arthur could hear.

'Ignore him,' Arthur replied, although the heckle continued.

'One swing from my sword should see that thing broken in two!'

Kay stopped walking.

'Kay,' Arthur warned. 'Don't–'

'My sword!' Kay gasped. 'I don't have my sword!'

'You– What?' Arthur was incredulous. Of all the things to forget!

'It's *your* fault!' Kay accused. 'You were supposed to bring it!'

'I–'

'What are you waiting for?' Kay demanded angrily. 'Go back and get it!'

Skidding on the wet mud, Arthur turned and fled back towards camp. Kay was right: it had been Arthur's job, as his squire, to bring the sword.

'Excuse me! Excuse me!' he cried, desperately trying to squeeze through the press of people. The crowd was growing

denser as the start of the tournament drew near, and everyone fought to get inside the arena. At this rate Arthur would be too late! By the time he got back with Kay's sword, Kay would have lost his chance to compete, and it would be all his fault.

Unless ...

An idea popped into Arthur's head – probably the stupidest he had ever had. But what choice was there?

With everyone flocking to the tournament grounds instead, it wasn't long before Arthur found himself in a deserted clearing, looking up at the sword in the stone.

Emrys had been right: it had called to him yesterday. He'd even seen it in his dreams.

Arthur glanced around, but he already knew he was alone. No one would be here until the tournament had finished. No one would know …

Cheering rose from the arena. The fighting was about to begin! Arthur scrambled over the rock, pulling himself up beside the sword.

Reaching out, he gripped the hilt. He felt instantly stronger. Stronger than he ever had before.

Without thinking, Arthur pulled, and without effort, the sword slipped free.

Just like that.

Arthur stumbled back, teetering atop the rock, and stared down at his hands.

He had done it! He had pulled the sword from the stone!

What did that mean?

The cheering came again, almost a roar. Then a metallic clash.

Arthur leapt from the rock, and ran towards the sound.

Kay was not where Arthur had left him. He was just inside the arena, now teaming with jousters and sword fighting, a bank of people on the far side standing and cheering them on.

Kay was arguing with a man who seemed to be on the brink of sending him to stand with the spectators or out on the street.

'This area is for contestants only!'

'Kay!' Arthur cried.

Kay spun around. When he spotted Arthur, he looked like a man who'd found water in the desert. 'You're here! I thought you'd never make it!' His relieved eyes fell on the sword in Arthur's hand. He looked again, and his jaw dropped. 'Is that …?'

Arthur nodded and offered it to him. 'Quick! Take it.'

Kay did not need to be told twice. He snatched the sword and held it aloft.

'He's got the sword!' a voice cried out.

Suddenly, Kay was surrounded by a crowd of people, with knights trailing squires still trying to dress them. Everyone wanted to see the sword and hear the story of how Kay had pulled it free.

'*Silence!*'

A strong voice bellowed above them all. Arthur turned to see Emrys striding towards them, Ector at his side. Ector gazed between his sons, a confused look on his face.

Emrys looked only at Kay. 'Are you really the one who freed the sword?'

Kay stood tall. 'Of course I am,' he retorted.

'Speak the truth, boy.'

Kay dropped his head. 'I am not,' he mumbled. Looking up, he pointed at Arthur. 'It was my brother, Arthur.' He held the sword out to Arthur. 'The sword is his.'

Arthur took it in a daze, and could have dropped it in shock when Kay knelt suddenly on one knee. Followed by Ector. Followed, one by one, by every man, woman and child in the arena.

Only Emrys remained standing, although he bowed deeply and smiled. 'At last,' he murmured. Then he lifted his staff and struck the ground.

A flash of light lit the backs of the kneeling crowd. By the time they squinted up from between their fingers, Emrys was gone. Or rather, the *old man* was gone.

Chapter Six

The tournament was over almost before it began. It wasn't needed anymore: the new king had been found. At first the people had seemed likely to swarm them in their excitement. Then Emrys had muttered something and they'd returned home instead. Quietly, dazedly – not unlike Arthur.

'I still don't understand,' he said back at camp, glancing at the now much younger man sitting opposite him, though still with the same gnarled staff. 'You're saying Ector is not my father?'

Ector answered for him. 'I'm sorry, Arthur, what Merlin says is true: I am not your father.'

Because Emrys wasn't Emrys either. He was a druid called Merlin.

And Arthur was ...

'Merlin brought you to me for protection when you were just a baby. He knew that I had a son of my own, not much older. He thought ...'

The words faded out. It was too much for Arthur to take in.

He looked at Kay, who hadn't spoken a word since Merlin had revealed Arthur's true heritage. He wanted to hear Kay tell him that nothing had changed. That no matter who his father was, Kay was still his brother.

'Arthur,' Merlin's voice broke through the fog in his mind. It was kind, but firm. 'You are Uther Pendragon's son and heir. Tomorrow you will come with me to Camelot, and claim your rightful place as King of Britain.'

'King of Britain,' Arthur repeated. Without a scabbard, the sword had been rolled into a blanket. He knew that it was nearby, but without seeing it he could almost pretend—

'It can't be true.'

Ector placed a hand on his shoulder. 'It is true, but it is not all that matters.' He forced Arthur to look at him. 'I may not be your father by blood, Arthur, but you will always be my son, no matter where life takes you.'

Arthur swallowed the lump in his throat. 'I want you to come with me. You and Kay.'

'You want *me* to come with you?' Kay asked, breaking his silence. 'Even after I tried to claim the sword for myself?'

'I can't be king without my brother by my side. If … If we are still brothers, that is …'

Kay stared at him. 'Of course we're still brothers!' he cried. 'Besides, who else will teach you how to use that sword?'

Arthur laughed. Just when it seemed that everything was changing, his family reminded him that some things never would.

And neither will I, Arthur resolved. *Wherever I sit, whatever I wear on my head, I'll always be a farm boy in my heart – only with a much bigger flock to take care of.*

Across the camp, Merlin smiled as if reading his thoughts – and perhaps he was. There was still so much that Arthur didn't know yet, but only one more thing that really mattered. They talked long into the night, but Arthur didn't ask that question. Only time would give him the answer.

The following day, Merlin led them into Camelot, the most beautiful place Arthur had ever seen. The castle was huge, with turrets towering into the sky at each corner of the outer wall. A vast stone bridge crossed a wide moat, leading up to an immense gatehouse. Beyond it was a courtyard bustling with people eager to see the new king. Arthur wasn't comfortable being the centre of so much attention, but he smiled through it all, thanking people for their kind words and promises.

Now he stood in an antechamber next to the Great Hall, dressed in clothes finer than even Kay could have dreamt of. A crest worthy of a king

glistened upon his tunic: three golden crowns.

He turned as Ector entered and bowed.

'You look like a true king,' Ector beamed. 'I know Uther would have been as proud as I am.'

'Did you know him?' Arthur asked. Ector's stories had been just that before. Now Arthur realised that they might have been memories instead.

Ector nodded. 'It was my honour to fight for him when I was younger.'

Arthur thought about the nicks and dents in Kay's sword.

'What kind of king was he?' Arthur asked, as he had done before when King Uther was just a character in a story. He cared so much more about the answer now.

'He was brave and strong,' Ector replied, also as before. Then he hesitated. 'And ruthless,' he added for the first time.

'Is he the reason you took me in?' Arthur wanted to know.

'He was my king and I wanted to serve him in any way I could. But I soon came to love you for yourself,' Ector assured him. 'Every bit as much as Kay.'

Arthur smiled and returned Ector's hug.

Behind them, the door opened and Kay stepped in, proudly wearing his own new crest: two white keys. He bowed. Then he teased, 'What has happened to my little brother? I hardly recognise you!'

Arthur felt more out of place than ever. 'I miss my farm clothes,' he muttered. He took a deep breath. 'I don't think I can do this, Kay.'

'Of course you can. You're Arthur Pendragon, King of Britain! You pulled the sword from the stone!'

Arthur wasn't sure that was enough, but he said nothing as the door opened again and Merlin appeared.

'Are you ready, Your Majesty?' he asked. 'Your people await.'

Ready or not, Arthur walked into the Great Hall, Merlin at his shoulder. The vast room was full of people who had come to see Arthur crowned. Catching sight of him, a hush fell over the hall as everyone knelt.

At the far end, on the dais, Arthur caught his first glimpse of the throne:

a large, straight-backed wooden chair, heavily carved with a red velvet seat. Uther Pendragon, strong, brave and ruthless, had sat on that throne. Now, as Arthur approached it himself, only one question filled his mind: *What kind of king will I be?*

CONTINUE THE QUEST WITH THE NEXT BOOK IN THE SERIES!

"This series opens the door to a treasure house of wonderful stories which have previously been available chiefly to older readers. We can only welcome it as a fabulous resource for all who love magical tales, and those who will come to love them."

JOHN MATTHEWS
AUTHOR OF THE RED DRAGON RISING SERIES AND ARTHUR OF ALBION